HAND TO MOUTH
BY DEBORAH SHELDON

A SHORT SHARP SHOCKS!
BOOK

BOOK 48

CONTENTS

HAND TO MOUTH

For Allen and Harry

April 7

James, I'm not a monster. First things first: despite reports to the contrary, I love your mother. Even now, after the terrible things she and I did to each other, my love remains unshakable. Relatives, police, lawyers, media (even those damned lab technicians) say otherwise, but I hope you'll believe me. Pray that you'll believe me. Consider this: when I've already lost everything, why would I bother lying to my own son? Especially about something so life-changing as the accident. This is my confession, written to you, the only person left who might listen.

Fair warning, you're not a child anymore so I won't keep back details in order to 'protect' you. In fact, since you'll be turning eighteen this year, I'll do my best forthwith to talk only man-to-man. (For the record, I'm not sure why our relationship has never been especially close, but I suspect it's because your mother is such a robust communicator. She did the talking for me. Do you consider me a distant father? If this is the case, I'm sorry, and I hope to make up for it with these letters. Yes, plural. I aim to write to you weekly. I have access to a laptop and a librarian helps me with the printer.)

James, I'll get straight to the point.

The day of the accident.

(This will be an honest account of what actually happened.)

We were driving from your grandmother's estate, having attended her seventy-fifth birthday soiree held in what I secretly call her 'back yard'. Ha ha. (Something I've never told you: I despise 'the terrace' with its topiaries and fountains. So vulgar.) The dress code was over the top, but the waiters in tails and the diamond-shaped ice sculpture shot the whole shindig into the upper stratosphere of ostentation. Of course, I said nothing to your mother but I knew she'd be watching me anyway for so much as a quirked eyebrow. In the end, I decided to be amused by the excesses of Matriarch's party. Well, you know your grandmother—never one to do anything by halves.

James, I had *not* been drinking. Check the police report. My blood alcohol reading was *zero*. Bottled mineral water the whole day. (And I hadn't taken any drugs either, despite the insinuations from relatives on your mother's side.) Whenever we socialise outside of our own house, your mother drinks and I don't. You remember that rule, don't you? It's inviolable. I swear on your own precious head: no alcohol and no drugs.

And yet, I can't explain the accident.

That's how rumours start: when the truth doesn't satisfy, people make up stories. Prior to that day, I'd never caused a bingle. In the thirty-plus years I've held my licence, I've been involved in just *four* motor vehicle accidents, and each time the other driver was at fault.

So, we were travelling along a dual-carriage highway. Green fields on either side. The hilly nature of the Yarra Valley causes roads to often dip and climb like rollercoaster tracks. The posted speed limit was 100 kilometres per hour, and yes, I was doing the speed limit *exactly*. I remember steering the car over an incline. The descent and subsequent rise promised a queasy, lurching sensation in the guts. The asphalt was dry. It had rained the night before, but the autumn sun had burned off the moisture. The sky shone blue with a few wispy clouds. No other traffic.

How to explain what happened next?

I drove the car over the incline. Your mother, who had been quaffing champagne, was in a spiky mood. Well, you know how she gets after a skinful. Agitated, prone to repeating herself. That's how she was that day. I didn't mind. After twenty-two years of marriage, you get used to mercurial moods. She's a passionate person, which is one of the reasons why I fell in love with her. Because opposites attract. She had such *zest* in her youth. Such feisty *zest*.

She said to me, "For Christ's sake, Graham, you ought to make more of an effort."

I said, "With your family? What do you mean? I thought I talked to everybody."

"No, you *greeted* everybody. There's a big difference."

According to the prosecution, that particular exchange constituted an *argument*. James, you know how it is between your mother and me, how it's always been? That 'exchange' was simply a discussion. No, not even a discussion—just normal, everyday conversation. Mundane stuff. After the relatives on your mother's side threw their weight around, minor details such as that conversation took on a disproportionate significance. Legal eagles saw *nuance* and *subtext* in our words but, driving home that day from Matriarch's soiree, there *was* no nuance or subtext. As usual, your mother wished that I had been more verbose at a social event and, as usual, I expressed hurt surprise. That's it. She's an extrovert while I'm an introvert. Case closed.

So, I steered the car down the incline at exactly 100 kph. The car reached the road's nadir. James, there was nothing there; no animal, no obstacle, *nothing*. The front wheels caught and bit. The car slung itself into a tree. (Strictly speaking, first took out a fence and then hit an old-man eucalypt, square on the front passenger door.) Your mother's arm took the impact. I remember the exclamation she made; a soft, disappointed and querulous 'ugh' sound, as if she had unexpectedly dirtied her hand.

Other sounds...the car crunching itself around the tree trunk, the smash of breaking glass, explosion of plastic shards. Then sirens. What I remember most, however, is the *ugh*.

Emergency lights. Staccato red and blue.

"My wife," I said, the strobes beating at my eyes. "Forget about me. Please help my wife."

The firemen had to cut the wreckage to get her out.

Memories of the hospital are vague. Cream walls. Smell of disinfectant. Chatter of nurses in the hallway. Beeping machine noises. Your mother and I were kept separate for days, perhaps weeks, or possibly the concussion befuddled my sense of time.

In any case, the hospital staff chose a dramatic way to reunite me with your mother. An orderly pushed my wheeled bed along corridors while a nurse kept pace, blathering about how I should *mentally prepare for God's plan* and that *things are bad, but they could have been much worse* and that I should *thank the Lord above for small mercies*. The nurse seemed upset. I stared down at my gold wedding ring and felt absolutely fine. Most likely on account of the painkilling medications; they fed pills to me every four hours whether I needed them or not. The trundling bed bumped over joins in the floor as we slogged from one wing into another. I remember thinking that the hospital must have grown in ungainly stages to keep pace with Melbourne's population. It's funny what you think about in times of great stress.

Your mother's face looked pale and flabby. When she saw me, she smiled with one side of her bruised mouth, tears streaming down her cheeks. Then she lifted her arms to me, as if for an embrace. Her bandaged left arm ended in a stump.

I have to go now. It's lights out.

<u>April 14</u>

James, my last letter was difficult to write. I expect this one will be too.

After I was discharged from hospital, they kept your mother for a further five weeks: one last week on the wards (in case of infection) with the balance at the Rehabilitation Centre. I visited her every day and brought Chardonnay smuggled in a thermos.

However, she had to schedule my visits so they didn't coincide with those of her relatives. They blamed me for what happened. In particular, Matriarch blamed me.

(Finally, Matriarch had a reason to justify her hatred. I'm sorry to disillusion you about your grandmother, James, but that stone-cold bitch loathed me from the moment we first locked eyes: over the dinner table during Christmas week. As a young man with a full head of hair, I'd been seeing your mother for a few months when your grandfather, Pa Rupert—you still remember him, don't you?—invited me to join them at the Yarra Valley estate for their traditional Boxing Day lunch. I didn't mind the old man; God rest his soul. Rupert shook my hand, proffered expensive Vouvray, seemed interested in my upcoming teaching post at the university. Matriarch glowered at me the whole time and didn't say a goddamned word. I think it disgusted her that I acknowledged the servants. Riddled with 'upstairs downstairs' prejudice, she considered me decidedly 'downstairs'. Ha ha. I'm not ashamed of my social standing. Intellect is considerably more valuable than wealth.)

But with regards to the accident, yes, as the driver of the vehicle at the time of the crash, technically the fault was mine. But not the *blame*. I didn't crash the car *on purpose*. That's an important distinction for you to understand. A distinction that the Court failed to make. (My lawyer wasn't competent. Too bad. I got what I was given because I didn't have the money to engage my own counsel. Your mother and I had joint bank accounts, and Matriarch made sure to freeze them all.)

On your head, James, I *swear* I didn't aim for the tree. Think about it: I'm not trained in stunt driving. I've puttered my sedan to and from work, keeping to the speed limit along back roads, ever since getting tenure in the English department, which was before you were even born. Twenty years! I don't know how to do a 'burnout' or a 'donut'. How could I have planned your mother's traumatic amputation? And in her own car, no less: the fancy Audi with its emphasis on driver-less technology.

I'm innocent, James.

Innocent.

I can only pray that you believe me.

When your mother came home from hospital, I was her willing serf. She would sit up in bed, resting against pillows I had plumped, and request camomile tea or wine or something very specific and particular for lunch, and I'd obey. She wanted *me* to tend to her; not our staff, not a hired nurse. And I would do *anything* for your mother. James, you *know* that to be true. Throughout our marriage, I've rubbed her feet and brushed her hair every night, and you're my witness to such attention, such utter devotion.

However, the *degree* of her helplessness surprised me at first. Then again, I'd never encountered such a disability before. It turns out there's not a lot you can do with only one arm. The littlest things were the most frustrating. For example, she couldn't unscrew a toothpaste tube. Pull on underwear or socks. Tie a shoelace. Open an envelope. Use a knife and fork. Do you see? Your mother felt like a newborn and frequently got upset. I assure you, I would've slaved for her tirelessly, without complaint, for the rest of her days.

The prosthetic was entirely Matriarch's idea.

James, I don't know how familiar you are with prosthetics, so here's my summary: once upon a time, an arm prosthetic was a dumb hunk of metal with a hook that had to be adjusted manually—switched to either 'closed' or 'open'—in order to work. Not so these days. Modern prosthetics can be wired to respond to your *nervous system*. You think 'open my hand' and the metal fingers open. You think 'make a fist' and the metal fingers close. Like a *real* hand. Disquieting stuff. Quite literally, the stuff of science fiction. Until a few years ago this technology was only the gleam in a fantasist's eye.

Of course, such advanced bio-robotics isn't available to just *anybody*. At least, not yet. No. It costs a toe-curling amount of money. And when it comes to toe-curling amounts of money, Matriarch has a few feet's worth. (Ha ha! There's a rather sophisticated

Dad Joke for you.) APRI—the Advanced Prosthetic Research Institute—received a one-million-dollar donation from Matriarch and then, miraculously, found a slot for your mother in its exclusive trial.

Oh, I shouldn't be so cynical. I'm grateful to Matriarch. Truly. The prosthetic was (at first blush) a *good thing* for your mother. It gave her hope. Focus. Purpose. If surgeon Dale Friedman hadn't made contact, your mother would have boozed herself to death, no doubt.

But did I resent the surgeries?

According to the prosecution, yes, because I wanted your mother to remain in my clutches. Let me explain. The surgeries were difficult. Painful. Exhausting. They demanded more than your mother could take. Many nights, I wept by her bedside as she suffered. None of that is in the court records. And do you know why? Because no one would take my word for it. The prosecution demanded *proof* of my state of my mind, but what proof could I offer? I don't keep a diary. They asked if I had ever recorded my tears and distress on my damned *phone*, as if I were some kind of angsty teenaged blogger. And no, I didn't confide in anyone, God forbid. (James, if you show your vulnerabilities, people use them against you; the urge to play little games of one-upmanship is an instinct hardwired into the human brain. Trust no one, I always say. Remember? If I taught you anything as a father, it was this basic principle.)

I'm rambling. I'm sorry. I still feel insulted, flabbergasted, blindsided by the court case.

Back to the surgeries. There were several, but the central aim was to relocate your mother's nerve endings.

How Dr Friedman explained it to me is how I'll explain it to you. Extending from the brain, three major nerves—the median, ulnar and radial—branch through the arm, down along the hand and into the fingertips. Even after amputation, these docked nerves may keep sending impulses that cause the brain to hallucinate the entire arm. That's why an amputee might feel 'pain' in their missing limb. So, the surgeries took those docked nerves from your mother's stump and stitched them into the skin of her shoulder.

After healing, if you pressed a spot on her shoulder, she felt it on her 'hand'.

In fact, the surgeons tattooed your mother's shoulder with coloured dots to show the relocation of her hand-nerves. Here's the map as I recall it:

- Black—thumb
- Blue—pointer
- Red—middle
- Yellow—ring
- Green—pinkie

After recovery, your mother was instructed to touch these dots multiple times per day to synchronise her brain with the relocated nerve endings. Whenever she was tired, which was often, I touched the spots on her behalf.

Doesn't sound scary on paper, does it, James?

But imagine touching a wheel of coloured tattoos on someone's shoulder while she says things like, "Ouch, don't pinch me," and "Let go of my finger," and "Why are you biting my thumbnail?" Imagine triggering a set of phantom digits which don't exist, and if that doesn't raise the hairs on your neck, you're a braver man than me. I used to dream about all of that. Have nightmares. For the first week or so, I slept in the spare room. Until your mother put her foot down, and insisted I return to the marital bed. Naturally, I had to comply.

Until my next missive. Take care.

<u>April 21</u>

James, now that I've started unburdening to you, I can't seem to stop. Am I oversharing? I wish you would reply to my letters. At the very least, I hope you're reading them.

The prosthetic. Dear God, the first time I saw it...

An avulsion injury is also known as 'degloving', which is a much more evocative term in my opinion. Have you heard of degloving? Picture a man riding a motorcycle at 80 kph along a bitumen road. He's dressed in a t-shirt and shorts instead of the recommended leathers. Now, if that man were to fall off at speed and slide along the road, he would slide at 80 kph, and the abrasive road surface would grip and evert his bare skin; meaning, rip it inside out. (And now you understand why I was opposed to you getting a motorcycle licence.)

'Degloved' is what sprang to mind when I first saw your mother's prosthetic appliance.

To be frank, it shocked me. *Repulsed* me. It resembled the skeletal structure of the arm but was instead coloured silver and black: titanium for the 'joints', carbon fibre for the 'bones'. Almost human but not quite. And *degloved*, for God's sake. Fleshless. Dr Ingrid Hofstadter (the APRI chief) had propped the appliance upright on her desk; the fingers splayed as if ready to catch a baseball, grip a waterglass, crush a face.

Oh, but your mother was *delighted*. She put her one remaining hand to her breast, and with eyes shining through unshed tears, gasped, "My goodness, Ingrid, it's just so *beautiful*."

Applause broke out. There were other staff members clustered in the room, all of them as happy and emotional as your mother. At least two saw my negative reaction and glared at me. (And later, testified against me in court.) But James, I wasn't upset at your mother's chance at independence. No! I was unsettled by the metal bones without muscles or skin, the fingers without fingernails, the goddamned precise and squared-off *lifelessness* of the appliance, its creepy mimicry of a living human arm. The *deglovement* of the infernal thing.

"Please, sit down," Ingrid invited your mother. "Let's see how things fit."

Above the titanium pretence of an elbow joint, the appliance ended in a socket. Ingrid fitted the socket over your mother's stump. Clicked the straps into place. Secured the 'receiver'—a flat, rubberised square of material—to your mother's shoulder, covering the black, blue, red, yellow and green tattoos that marked the nerves of her missing fingers. Dizzy, I needed to sit but there was no spare chair. The two staff members kept fixing me with suspicious eyes. I tried to smile, to appear normal and joyful at the occasion, but...I had psychological trauma too. Didn't I count? For some reason, no, I didn't. Everyone ministered and fawned over your mother, but no one gave me a moment's thought. It was then, during that appointment, I first suspected Matriarch of paying for more than just the prosthetic.

"How does that feel?" Ingrid said.

Your mother smiled. "Perfect."

With the appliance fitted, she became something else: a sci-fi robot, a hybrid machine-monster. And that was even before Ingrid activated the ON switch. My skin crawled. I knew I would never want to touch your mother again. *Not ever again*.

Ingrid turned to her computer monitor, hovered over the keyboard.

My breath caught. I recalled the car accident, and wished that my body had hit the tree instead. That I had died instead.

"Here we go," Ingrid said, and pressed a sequence of keys.

The appliance made a faint and anticlimactic sound, akin to the hum of a faraway hair dryer. I almost laughed. Your mother actually *did* laugh, blurting out a shrill bray of surprise.

"Good God, I can feel it!" she said. "A vibration. Is it alive?"

Ingrid said, "Focus as practised. Shut your eyes if you prefer. Now. Close your hand."

On tenterhooks, every muscle in my body tensed for flight. I couldn't blink. I gaped at the appliance. At the flat, matt shine of its fake bones and pretend fingers.

Seconds passed. The robo-thumb moved. A single twitch.

Your mother choked and gulped. The staff whooped.

My heart spasmed. A buzzing noise knocked inside my skull.

Next, when the robo-digits clenched in concert, I broke from the room and found myself in a corridor, panting, retching. The technician who tugged at my arm was a young man with long blonde hair. *I'm not lying*. And I didn't imagine him either. The police never found him, APRI denied his existence, but he was real. He tugged at my sleeve. His eyes were wide. *Frightened*. Other things about him I recall: crooked front teeth, a long and pointed chin. I offered to describe him to a sketch artist. My offer was promptly rebuffed. They didn't want to *hear* my side of the story, James. What does that tell you?

The technician said, "They can program the appliance. To do anything they want."

Dazed, all I could reply was, "I'm sorry?"

"Listen. The remote control for making resets and adjustments is also a conduit for covert instructions. There's Trojan horses. Malware that can backdoor into the software. I helped write the programs. Watch yourself."

The young man hurried away. By the time others emerged from Ingrid's office in pursuit of me, I was alone. Contrary to court records and the sworn testimony of every single member of the APRI staff including the director Ingrid Hofstadter, the mysterious technician whom no one can identify *was* real, and I believe what he told me to be the truth: *your mother's appliance was hacked*.

Soon after the fitting, the appliance attacked me for the first time.

Your mother was in the lounge room, reclined on the couch and tucked under a blanket. I had just brought out her lunch: one sandwich and another glass of wine. I put the lunch next to her on the coffee table. The prosthetic appliance, as usual, was humming. (I had taken to whistling so that I wouldn't have to focus on its ceaseless noise.)

I said, "I'll help you with your exercises later. I need to prepare for tomorrow's lecture."

"Oh, *sure* you do," she said in her drunken, sarcastic sing-song voice. "Uh-huh. Okay. No worries."

She's always been the jealous type, remember? She resented my working from home; she considered it my duty to give full attention to her whenever I was within those walls, and that was even *before* she lost her arm.

I tried to ignore her tone. "I'll be in the study."

"Ringing Amy, I suppose."

"Well, why not? She's my tutor. We have to consult—"

"*Consult?* Is that what you're calling it?" Your mother sneered. "You son of a bitch."

The appliance hit me across the face. During the trial, the technicians were adamant that the appliance can only move slowly, tediously, deliberately. I'm telling you, it hauled off and belted me in the wink of an eye, so fast I hardly saw it coming.

The blow split my lip. I staggered. Held a hand to my bleeding mouth.

Rapt, your mother stared at the appliance in awed reverence. "It read my mind. How extraordinary. I wanted to slap you and it actually *read my mind*."

"So, from now on, any physical abuse won't be your fault anymore, is that the implication?" Bristling with sudden anger, I whispered through my teeth, "Don't push me."

She regarded me for a time, as if committing my features to memory, and then she smiled. "If I ever wanted to kill you, Graham, I'd never be imprisoned for it or even arrested. You know why? Because I'd tell the police that you beat me. That you'd beaten me for years and years, and I was terrified of you; too afraid to ever tell anybody or seek help. And I would be believed. Because I'm a woman. And you're a man."

I felt cold, sick. "You're exactly like your goddamned mother."

"Do you see how it is, Graham? How it's going to be?"

I hung my head. "Yes. I see."

"Ring Amy," she said, using the robo-hand to pick up her wine, "and break things off."

And I did. (For the record, Amy was indeed my lover, but that's not the point I'm trying to make here.)

Until next time, James. All my love.

<u>April 28</u>

I'm sorry, James. What I told you in my last letter was a fabrication. Not all of it—just the last part, the argument with your mother. That particular argument never happened. It's the same story I told in court, under oath, a story that my lawyer and I concocted in an attempt to sway the jury. However, the story isn't so much a *lie* as a *distillation*. For example, your mother *had* threatened me using similar words, but it was many years ago and she was playing around; only teasing, I think. She didn't mean anything. Not at that stage, at least.

Hand on heart, I included the story because the prison administration reads my letters (hello, Governor!) and I was afraid to contradict my testimony. But God, what kind of father would I be if I cared more about an additional charge of perjury than telling the truth to my own son? Forgive me. I promise to be nothing but honest. As honest as I can possibly be.

It's true the accident changed our marriage. Not for the better, of course. How could it?

The three main reasons for the change:

1. I felt riddled with guilt, consumed and tortured by it. After all, I'd been driving the car.

2. Your mother resented me, blamed me. Oh, she tried to hide it, but I could discern traces of bitterness in her voice, her manner, in the way I'd catch her looking at me. I tried to talk with her about this, but she denied every accusation. Would spend an inordinate amount of time attempting to reassure me. *The lady doth protest too much, methinks.* Yet, sometimes, she almost had me convinced I was imagining things.

3. Her family, headed by Matriarch, began a slur campaign. They wanted me charged with various crimes including, but not limited to, your mother's attempted murder. Their constant insinuations wore your mother down in the end. That's what I tell myself, anyway. She wasn't in her right mind. You mustn't hold any ill will towards your mother.

While she was meant to use the appliance during waking hours, your mother also had a program of daily exercises to perform. The program entailed a set list of manipulation attempts. Typically, she would sit at the kitchen table and I'd arrange the prerequisite items for her to pick up, manipulate and put down. These items ranged from the relatively easy to grasp (such as a tennis ball) to the increasingly more challenging (such as pens and even paperclips). The strain made her puff and sweat as if she were running a marathon. I'd rate her performance in the journal, which APRI staff perused at a later date.

James, doesn't my cooperation, my willingness to help, prove my love for your mother? Because watching the appliance never failed to make my flesh creep. It resembled a real hand but didn't move like one, and the joints used to *click*. In the evenings, reading in my study, I'd often hear that *click* and have to check the hallway to convince myself that I was alone and safe.

The next time your mother hurt me was during one of these exercise programs. She picked up a pencil and stabbed me with it. *Bang*. Straight into my wrist. Plunged with enough force to stick the pencil fast. (A piece of lead broke off. To this day, if you part the hairs you can see the dark grey smudge through my skin.)

Your mother shrieked. As did I. We both jumped up from the table and regarded the pencil stuck in my arm. I pulled it out. There was a surprising amount of blood. While I rinsed the wound under the running tap, your mother swore to me—James, she *swore* to me—that she hadn't planned or intended the stabbing. That the appliance had done it. And I took her words at face value.

Naturally, we brought up the incident at our next appointment with Dr Ingrid Hofstadter.

"I know you want answers but I can't explain what happened," she said. "We've run the diagnostics. We can't find any evidence of a malfunction."

"Perhaps it wasn't a malfunction," I said, remembering my encounter with the young, frightened technician, an encounter I'd kept to myself at that stage of the game. "Perhaps the appliance was simply following its backdoor programming."

They both stared at me as if I were mad.

"You believe," Ingrid said at last, "that we programmed the appliance to *stab* you?"

"I believe," I said, "that firstly, my mother-in-law has bribed APRI—indirectly, of course—with a grotesque amount of money for this device, and secondly, that everybody has a price."

Your mother gripped my leg, *hard*, with the robo-hand. "Graham, for Christ's sake..."

"I don't understand," Ingrid said.

"Software Trojan horses," I continued, voice rising. "Covert instructions to finish me off."

"Wait a minute, you think I'm some kind of paid *assassin*?"

"I think you'll do whatever it takes to keep receiving cheques from my mother-in-law."

Ingrid was a convincing actress; I'll give her that. She looked both stunned and insulted. Then she turned to your mother and said, "Is your husband receiving psychiatric support?"

Which is how the slander got started. Bankrolled by Matriarch. Why everyone now thinks I'm unbalanced. Yet the besmirching is a smokescreen. To hide the truth: Matriarch wanted me out of the way because she decided from the get-go—from the very first Boxing Day lunch with Grandpa Rupert—that

I'm with your mother solely for her inheritance.

But consider the facts. We've been together twenty-five years. *A quarter century*. If I was in it for the money, good God, then I've been playing quite the long con, haven't I? Therefore, purely from a logical point of view, Matriarch's hypothesis is *insane*. And why drag my poor tutor, Amy, into this delusion? Well, because doing so further helps to smear my reputation. Do you see?

Oh, James, how people *love* juicy gossip. And me trying to murder your mother in a car crash in order to become a rich playboy and elope with my younger lover? Ha ha! So juicy!

And untrue, I might add. Untrue and wicked. (Although, as the prosecution pointed out, it would be fair to say that, on my salary alone, I couldn't possibly maintain the lifestyle to which I was accustomed. In my opinion, it was this fact that swayed the jury into swallowing the prosecution's entire hare-brained theory about my motives.)

I'm in jail solely because the average person likes to believe salacious gossip.

Damn, the unfairness makes me gnash my teeth, rip my hair.

Everyone is against me. Everyone!

Oh God, James! God! The noise in this place after dinner is unbearable. Confined to their cages, the men are beasts, shouting and hollering and shrieking. A madhouse. I'm sitting here on my cot, weeping. James, I'm not sharing this information to curry sympathy. How could I fool you? Such a smart boy. You've *always* been a smart boy. I couldn't have asked for a better child. A better son. James, oh James, I'm sorry.

For everything, for all things.

Please. I need you to forgive me.

I promise, I never meant for *any* of this to happen.

Sometimes, I lie awake at night and mentally retrace every step that brought me here, to this cell, to this tiny cell with its flat, lumpy mattress, vandalised walls, metal toilet. The answer is the same: *the prosthetic*. But your mother accused me of paranoia. She said that the appliance, being experimental, still had bugs to iron out; that the odd occasion when it would turn on me without warning to pinch or twist or punch were nothing but glitches. *That's why we keep going back to the lab for updates*, she would tell me, *to fix these glitches and fine-tune its programming.*

And at times, lying here in the dark, I believe her. It could be that my revulsion for the appliance, and my suspicion of Matriarch, skewed my interpretation of what was actually going on. Perhaps I connected the dots when a few of the dots weren't really there.

Tell me, James. Which version of the truth do you find more plausible?

The version put forward by the prosecution? Or mine?

<u>May 5</u>

James, we never had *The Talk*, did we? About the birds and the bees. Another failing of mine as a parent. I could never seem to find the right time or opportunity to bring up such an embarrassing topic. (To be honest, I thought your mother would've had that conversation with you, or that you would learn about the mechanics of sex during Health Education at school. Did either of those things happen? I'm sorry to say I have no idea.)

So now, without having ever broached the topic, I'm about to tell you about Amy.

Contrary to what was stated in the trial, our affair wasn't 'sordid'. As you know, she was the tutor for my classes. Therefore, we shared a lot in common: a love of language, poetry, literature and etymology, just for starters. Amy was almost my intellectual equal. (And yes, while your mother has her endearing traits, intelligence isn't one of them. Opposites attract, is how I would explain it. Your mother has passion. *Zest*. And a temper, let's not forget. A temper that was very fetching in her youth; less so in middle age, particularly when booze would give it that hard, sniping edge. She liked to go for the jugular. Never show anyone your weak spots, James, or you'll see them used against you. Mark my words.)

Amy was intelligent, yes. And attractive in a strait-laced 'librarian' kind of way. (Not that she wore glasses or her hair in a bun.) Picture a slim, demure woman with minimal makeup, unpainted nails, sensible clothing, flat shoes. The kind of cool understatement that suggests a possibility of sexual heat simmering beneath—if coaxed to the surface in the right way. A clichéd fantasy? Yes, there's probably a category for that kind of thing on pornography websites. (I apologise for my frankness, and hope I'm not making you too uncomfortable.)

But James, her cool façade is what first piqued my interest, because I speculated about her repressed, hidden, *carnal* possibilities. And yes, oh God, she was *young*. Twenty years my junior. The vanity of a man well past his prime can't be overestimated.

I've lost most of my hair, my belly has grown soft, limbs thinner, chest saggier—and yet I was desired! By an intelligent, attractive, youthful woman! She sought out my company. Laughed at my jokes. Held my gaze for a few seconds too long. It got so that I couldn't stop thinking about her. I fantasised about touching her, kissing her. And more, of course. Much more...

Naturally, I felt guilty. Breaking the marital vows that one makes in church, before God and family, is a terrible thing. But I felt alive for the first time in years! Sharing any details would be grossly inappropriate (and sickening for a son to hear), so I'll give you this brief summary: when it came to sexual congress, your mother was reticent; Amy was enthusiastic. There. That's all you need to know to understand my extended period of weakness.

Did your mother know? She suspected. Did she share those suspicions with Matriarch? Yes, I believe she did. And Matriarch wanted me out of the picture, to keep the Old Money safe from my clutches in case of divorce. James, can you see how the threads are tying together?

They put Amy on the stand. Initially, I thought she would be a witness for the defence, but no, no. The prosecution asked her questions, and her answers put me in a bad light.

Q: Did the defendant ever suggest the possibility of you running away together?

A: Yes.

Q: How many times? Once? Twice?

A: Many times. Dozens of times.

James, it was agony to see Amy up there, testifying against me, never meeting my eye. I remember shaking, feeling dizzy. My lawyer asked for a recess, but the judge wouldn't allow it. Once, I'm sure that damned judge looked behind me, to where Matriarch was sitting, and actually *smiled*. Collusion once again. *Money talks*.

Q: Did the defendant offer any plan as to how the two of you would run away?

A: (loaded silence and fidgeting; oh, Amy put on quite a show for the prosecution.)

Q: Please answer the question. How did the defendant plan to leave his wife for you?

A: Um, he mentioned the possibility of her maybe...dying.

Q: His wife? *Dying?* (approaching the jurors with open arms) And was his wife *ill* at this point? Was anything *wrong* with her medically? Had she been diagnosed with terminal cancer? Dementia? Anything of that nature, to your knowledge?

A: No.

Q: And let's be clear; this is *before* the defendant caused the car accident, which didn't take her life but took her limb.

My lawyer: Objection!

Judge: Overruled! The witness may answer the question.

A: Yes, this was before the car accident.

Q: When you heard about the accident, what was your conclusion?

A: I don't understand the question.

Q: Okay, let me put it another way: did you believe the car crash was actually an accident?

My lawyer: Objection!

Judge: Overruled!

A: I wasn't sure if it was an accident. All I knew was that Graham often wished his wife dead, so I guess...I wasn't surprised to hear about the crash.

God, and on and on the smear campaign went. James, can't you see the obvious truth? *Matriarch paid Amy to lie.* There's no other explanation. Well, either paid her off or threatened her life. I'm not being paranoid here. Pay careful attention: Amy was *in love* with me. She had said so, often, and not just while lying in my arms, giddy with post-coital hormones. She had whispered it at work too. In the corridors as we passed, she liked to brush her fingers against my hand. She loved me wholeheartedly, unreservedly, wildly.

But did I love her back?

Well, in retrospect, it's hard to say. With twenty years between us in age, there's a generation gap that can't be bridged. Her taste in music was dubious. She was a fan of 'memes', which I never found amusing. Social media platforms didn't interest me in the same way they interested her. And James, to be honest, I still loved your mother. We shared history. We shared *you*. We understood each other in ways that Amy and I never could.

However, I *did* talk with Amy about leaving your mother. That part is true. You see, Amy liked to pipe dream. In particular, she enjoyed picturing our future home: a middling two-bedroom apartment somewhere in the dreary outer-eastern suburbs of Melbourne.

Yes, that's the meagre size of mortgage we could have afforded. A lecturer and a tutor at a third-rate university hardly enjoy stellar wages, and real estate is expensive. So, James, my admission is that your private school education, our live-in staff, the twice-yearly holidays at our various European properties—in fact, every privilege you've enjoyed since birth—have all been paid for by your mother's side of the family. But I suppose you knew that already.

(However, I don't feel *sorry* for myself. God, do you think I'm upset because your mother's side of the family is filthy rich? Not in the slightest. Money is cheap, available everywhere in any society that maintains a reasonable economy. Consider this: what use is a university without lecturers? No use at all. Therefore, the rich fee-paying families are the minions that serve the king, ergo, the lecturer. It is the *lecturer* with his skillset that holds the power. Not Matriarch with her money. Do you understand? *Skill* is what counts.)

Talking about our mythical two-bedroom apartment in a blue-collar suburb enthralled Amy, but had the exact opposite effect on me: it took the shine off our affair. The more Amy wittered on about me leaving your mother, the more reluctant I became about doing so.

Jealousy. Perhaps *that's* why Amy testified against me. Not because of money or fear.

Let me explain further.

One day, Amy gave me an ultimatum. In my office. She said she wanted a baby. *My* baby. She wasn't getting any younger, our affair wasn't just 'mucking around', etc. I demurred, pointing out that I was married already, had a near-grown son, couldn't imagine at my age the rigmarole of nappies, late nights, swimming lessons, or life in a small apartment with one car between us and no European holidays. Amy's response to my reasonable refusal?

Threats.

That she would report me to the police, to the Dean, to your mother. In short, destroy me in every way she could think of unless I freed myself to marry her and sire her child. Oh, it's a mistake to trust people, James. As a general rule, people only look out for themselves. Remember that.

Stalling, I told Amy I needed time to think.

Upon reflection, perhaps she didn't lie on the stand because of Matriarch's influence. Perhaps Amy lied solely because she wanted to make good on her threat: to destroy my life. And destroy it she did. I could actually *see* the impact her testimony had on the jury. The men and women scowled at me with open hostility. Amy, light of my life, besmirched me for her own selfish ends. Or because Matriarch had paid her or intimidated her—look, I can't decide which scenario is more likely.

You're a smart boy, James. I can't fob you off. The central question remains and I know you're wondering about it: had I ever discussed with Amy the possibility of running away with her *if your mother happened to die?*

The answer is...yes.

But I hasten to add, it was nothing but idle speculation, *not* an admission that I would try to kill her in a car accident. Look, your mother drinks too much, is grossly overweight, never exercises, has a penchant for *foie gras* and other such fatty, artery-clogging foods. And she's menopausal. A heart attack is not beyond the realms of possibility. And *that* was how I framed your mother's death. I swear it. As a pie-in-the-sky dream. Like winning the lottery. It was *not* a promise. Whatever Amy surmised, I never promised that your mother would die.

I have to stop here. The guards want to search our cells.

<u>May 12</u>
James, it's taken me a long time to tell you exactly what happened on that fateful night.

I've tried to provide crucial background information first so that you can grasp the *actualities*. Please, set aside everything you may have read in the newspapers. Forget the sensationalist details of the trial. The podcasts, the theories, the fascination.

Please *listen to me*.

First things first: I appreciate that the revelations about my relationships with your mother and Amy may have come as a shock. Before I wrote these letters, I'm sure you would have described your mother and I as a *happy couple*. This was how we had decided to present our marriage to you. It was our tacit agreement. Unless you've had a child yourself, James, you can't appreciate the degree of pretence that an outwardly-successful marriage requires. Who wants to damage their son (or daughter) with the truth? Not us! Your mother and I weren't especially happy but we *weren't* especially unhappy either. Most marriages are like that. Unfulfilling. Try to understand. Once the honeymoon period is over (and it lasts about, oh, I would guess about five years), it's a long and anaesthetising grind to the bitter end.

Surprise! My marriage wasn't ideal. So what?

Okay, James, I'm being honest now.

And keep in mind that your mother's prosthetic arm kept *hurting* me. Tried to *kill* me on more than one occasion. Quite often, I think it was simply doing your mother's bidding, whether she was conscious of it or not. Other times, I've no doubt that at least one technician at APRI, having been paid off by Matriarch, was programming the arm. (Probably that bitch Dr Ingrid Hofstadter.) The truth must lie in one theory or the other.

Or both? It's hard to say.

I can't prove either theory beyond a reasonable doubt—which is why I'm languishing in prison—but I swear to you that everything I've told you in my letters so far is true, or as near to the truth as I can make it.

So, the fateful night in question...

Look, as you know, your mother has various sleep difficulties. Insomnia, for one. And she is occasionally afflicted by dreams about being attacked. By dogs, usually. Or lions, sharks, spiders—any creature that's frightening. Strictly speaking, these dreams are more than just nightmares. They are episodes of *night terrors* and the dreams feel *real* to her. She thrashes to defend herself. Many times, I've shaken her arm or called out to her, and copped more than a few kicks to my legs over the years. Usually, she wakes up confused and distressed for the first few seconds until she realises that the danger was only a dream. Then she apologises. It's not an issue. I've never held these episodes against her.

James, do you remember the incident when you were about twelve? Your mother was attacking me. I was yelping in pain. You ran into our bedroom, turned on the overhead light, and yelled, "What the hell is going on?" Your voice woke up your mother. She cried when she saw the blood on my face. Remember? Do you remember, James? Yes, of course you do. How could you forget? It affected your sleep for weeks afterwards. You kept worrying that your mother would attack me again. One time, you actually said to me, "Dad, what if she tries to kill you?" Out of the mouths of babes...

Soon after the prosthetic arm was fitted, your mother took to wearing it overnight. That seemed crazy to me. Like wearing dentures, contact lenses or corrective shoes in bed; why on earth would you? But the staff at APRI—and in particular, Dr Ingrid Hofstadter—kept suggesting that your mother *never* remove the prosthetic. That she should consider it *as her own arm*. Ostensibly, to faster train the software. (Ultimately, they planned to permanently affix the prosthetic—or more precisely, its next generation model—into the bone of her upper arm. Meaning, drill and bolt the damned thing. Christ, just the thought of that makes me ill.) But asking her to wear the prosthetic at all times, apart from when showering, smacked to me of another, more sinister agenda.

The prosthetic hummed at night.

Kept me awake.

The robo-arm would often rise into the air, fingers working and flexing, even while your mother snored, drunk and dead to the world. Was she dreaming and moving her arm in her sleep? Or was the robo-arm responding to commands from a corrupted APRI technician?

This one terrible night I'm talking about, somewhere around 2AM, the violent flapping of bedclothes startled me awake. I looked over. Your mother was sitting up, dimly lit by our electric clock, wrenching frantically at the bedlinen and kicking, as if reacting to the scratch of huntsman spiders or cockroaches swarming in their hordes over her bare legs.

"What is it?" I said, and pulled out an earplug. (I'd taken to wearing earplugs at night; otherwise, I couldn't sleep for the humming.)

Your mother didn't answer me. Instead, her thrashing became more frenzied. Something was in the bed with her, scaring her, and my heart rate kicked up.

Panicked, I yelled, "What's going on?" and reached out.

Remember, James, I was lying prone and your mother was sitting upright. At the sound of my voice, she turned to me, wrenched the bedclothes away in both hands—one real, one monstrous—and then began to beat me. Silently, without a word. I screamed. Her flesh-and-bone fist was nothing more than a tap, but the prosthetic fell on me as weighty as a hammer.

"Wake up!" I yelled. "You're attacking me, wake up!"

No good. Your mother redoubled her efforts. The prosthetic pummelled me. A rib bone broke. The agony was terrible, and took my breath. I lifted my hands in an attempt to defend myself against the onslaught, until the smash of the prosthetic crumpled my fingers. I rolled out of bed. Leapt to my feet, panting, frightened.

Your mother leapt out of bed too.

"Wake up!" I shrieked, as she came for me, robo-fingers clacking.

And now, after all is said and done, I believe that your mother knew what she was doing. She was trying to murder me. Whether she hated me because of the car accident or because of Amy or a combination of both, the end result was the same: *your mother tried to murder me.*

Check the police reports. No one disputes that your mother had experienced night terrors in the past. No one disputes that the prosthetic had glitches. But here's where the narrative becomes blurred: how your mother died. According to the police and prosecution, I took the lamp from my bedside table and stoved in her head, but that's not what happened.

What happened was that the prosthetic closed its degloved fingers around my throat and squeezed. I felt pain. A terrible pressure within my cranium, behind my eyes. Blackness encroached on my vision. It occurred to me that I was dying.

I was prone on the floor. Your mother was sitting on top of me. I grabbed something—as it turned out, the metal door-stopper, the one shaped like a rooster—and hit her with it. One strike. Not to kill her, you understand, but simply to get her off me, to stop her prosthetic arm from choking me to death.

But as it turned out, the door-stopper knocked her unconscious. That damned rooster door-stopper I'd always despised (but your mother insisted was her absolute favourite out of all the ornaments crowding every surface in the bedroom) had cracked her skull. She fell onto her side and lay still. I thought it was over, that I was safe.

The prosthetic, clacking and whirring, rose up and again clamped its cold metal fingers on my windpipe. Yes, I wrestled with the damned thing. Yes, I got to my feet and, using all my strength, wrenched it from your mother's stump. And as it fought me with superhuman power, this degloved and amputated monstrosity, I believed in my panic that your mother's thoughts still directed it. And *that's* why I brought it down on her head. Terrified, I thought she was playing possum, only feigning unconsciousness, and that I had to knock her out *for real* in order to save myself.

Yes, James, I bludgeoned her to death. May God forgive me, I kept whipping her with the full weight of the prosthetic, over and over, while it hummed and whirred and clenched its fingers, twisting, attempting to grab me. When the infernal thing finally switched off, becoming locked and rigid, I stopped too. Threw the disgusting thing away from me. It clattered across the floorboards and I stared at it in horror, expecting it to right itself and begin crawling and scrabbling towards me. After long minutes, when it didn't move, I finally looked down at your mother.

And saw her brain tissue.

James, I'm crying right now. Bawling like a newborn. This letter has taken me the best part of a day to write. I'm not sure if I've adequately captured my shock, my confusion, on that awful night. I never intended to kill her. I swear to you. I swear on your precious head. I love you, James. Oh, my son, my only son. My only child. I'm so sorry. Can you forgive me? Can you ever find it in your heart to forgive me? All I can do is pray. Cry and pray for your forgiveness, tonight and every night, for the rest of my miserable life.

<u>May 19</u>

I've been talking in circles these past weeks. Round and round and round...

You know it, and I know it.

James, do you remember when you were little and questioned me about Santa

Claus? That particular evening, we had put up the Christmas tree. You, me and your mother. We'd festooned that stinking pine with lights and tinsel, with your mother's expensive trinkets, and the lovely paper ornaments you'd made at kindergarten. Afterwards, I'd tucked you into bed. And you'd blindsided me by asking, "Daddy, is Santa real?"

Now, keep in mind, you were only four. (You were a smart boy right from birth; verbal at such an early age. So curious about the world. Intellectually, a veritable *sponge*.) And children are supposed to believe in Santa Claus, the Easter Bunny and the Tooth Fairy etc. until they are at least six years old, apparently, or perhaps even seven. For God's sake, I didn't know what to *say*. Your mother was busy in the kitchen pouring herself another slug, and the staff had retired for the night. James, I was at a loss. With nowhere to turn, I tried to stall with generic blather.

"As long as there are children," I began, "and as long as there is Christmas, there will always be Santa Claus because he embodies the spirit of the season." I still think it's a good answer, and one that should have satisfied you. (But then, I shouldn't have underestimated you. James, my smart little boy, ever sharp as a tack.)

"But is Santa *actually* real?" you insisted.

"Yes."

"As real as I am? I mean, could I see him? Touch him? Could he pick up this teddy bear?"

"Well," I said at last, trying to chuckle. "I'm not sure. After all, he's a magical being."

"You told me magic isn't real."

Because of that blasted pantomime with the wicked witch getting crushed to death. God, it gave you such nightmares. I had to explain—over and over—that 'magic' was nothing but lies, deception, sleight of hand, smoke and mirrors. Via the Internet, I even showed you how a few tricks were done. Your mother accused me of stealing your *Childhood Innocence*, but I saw it as offering you reassurance in an uncertain world. And that scene from the pantomime no longer gave you nightmares, which means I did the right thing. Didn't I?

Regarding Santa, I tried to fudge the issue, replying, "Some types of magic might be real."

Oh, James, you fixed me with your sideways stare. The stare I came to know very well over the years; the look that means you're sniffing what you term as *bullshit.* "Magic is real or it's not," you declared.

"Yes," I sighed. "Very true."

"Is Santa real?"

"I can't tell."

"How does Santa get the presents to every house in the world in one night?"

"I don't know," I said.

"There's no chimney. How does he get inside *our* house?"

"I don't know."

"Does he break in? Is he a bad guy?"

"No. Stop. Please."

That side-eye again. You said, "Is he real? Like me? *Alive* like me? Don't lie, Daddy."

I sat on the edge of the bed and took your hand. It was so small and warm. I can still recall the wriggle of your fingers against my palm. I said, "What I'm about to tell you, you can't tell your mother. Or any of your friends at kindergarten."

Your eyes widened and you sucked in your breath. "All right."

"This has to be our secret."

You nodded.

And I told you the truth. You were pleased, actually. Happy that you had already figured it out. And I was so proud of you. My smart little boy. And you never told your mother or, as far as I'm aware, your friends either. The farce of Santa Claus remained our secret.

Often, this memory wakes me up.

Like everybody else, I keep secrets from myself. We all do. Reality is *painful*. We couch ourselves as the 'good guy'. That instinct is hardwired into the Ego. Does a criminal ever define himself as evil? Does he ever see himself as justified in his actions, as some kind of hero righting a wrong, as a rebel sticking it to The Man? Possibly. In all likelihood, I'm as blind to my own actions as the dumbest of dumb criminals. I don't know, *I don't know*.

But here's a bit of insight.

There's another reason why your mother may have wanted to kill me.

And to be honest, I can't really blame her. I've thought about killing myself, many times. If I had the guts, the wherewithal, I probably would have done it by now.

Oh God...drawing breath is difficult. My hands are shaking, eyes filling with tears. Nevertheless, I have to go on. Do I have the strength to tell you? We'll see. No more games.

Let's return all the way back to the first letter I wrote: about Matriarch's soiree at her Yarra Valley estate. We were there to celebrate her seventy-fifth birthday. Us and about two hundred other people. (That bitch collects hangers-on like stamps.) Once again for the record, I didn't have anything to drink and I hadn't consumed any drugs. Naturally, your mother was soused and angry by the time we were driving home. Along that rollercoaster road in the Yarra Valley. With nothing to hit.

Green fields. Me behind the wheel. A speed of 100 kilometres per hour.

I still don't know what happened.

The buck of your mother's Audi, the punch through the fence and that sideways slew into the old-man eucalypt, the disappointed *ugh* sound your mother groaned as her door crumpled itself around the tree and the twisting metal pulped her forearm.

Emergency lights. Staccato red and blue.

"My wife," I said, the strobes beating at my eyes. "Forget about me. Please help my wife."

James, I only said that because when I looked into the back seat, you weren't there. I wasn't thinking straight. I had concussion. For some reason, I thought you were at home, playing one of your online games with your mates. I forgot—for a quite a while, actually—that you had been with us at Matriarch's soiree, grinning sarcastically with that slight roll of your eyes at everyone's gasping exclamation about how much you'd *grown* since the last soiree, the one celebrating Matriarch's seventy-fourth birthday.

And when I remembered, red and blue lights flashing, that you had been in the back seat, I thought your absence meant that you were strolling around outside the wreck, hands in your pockets, slouching, huffing with impatience. You wanted to get home, of course. You had a *game* scheduled, of course. No wonder you'd be annoyed. Pissed off with me. I was forever thwarting your online plans for various reasons that weren't my fault, such as social events requiring the whole family. But I couldn't have cared *less* about all that rubbing-shoulders stuff and nonsense. Honestly, I didn't care! Like you, James, I preferred to stay home and keep my own counsel.

Bleeding, I remember saying to one of the firemen, "Tell James to let his mates know he'll be late. Maybe they can reschedule the game."

"James?" the fireman said, and his eyes were very blue. "Who's that? Your son?"

"Why, yes. He's a keen gamer. Very keen."

The fireman gripped my shoulder. I didn't understand why. I gazed out through the shattered windscreen and wondered why the fireman was gripping my shoulder so tightly.

"Can you tell him?" I said. "Tell him to let his mates know."

The fireman left my side of the car. Everything went black. I woke up in the hospital. The painkilling drugs made life a soft, gentle dream. I remember seeing your mother's stump, and being told by somebody—a priest, a police officer, a doctor?—about your death. Apparently, without a seatbelt, you were shot through the windscreen. Broken, you landed in a roadside ditch. None of these details about you sank in at first. Over the subsequent weeks and months, life moved in a sideways, otherworldly blur that didn't make much sense. You were gone from the house, the staff never spoke of you, and I didn't understand why. Then I killed your mother. No, *defended* myself against your mother.

I'm so tired. I try to eat. Food turns to ashes in my mouth. I'm losing weight. My trousers are baggy; I hold the waist of them in my fist. I have no friends here.

So, James, I write you these letters. I post them to our home address and they get returned to me in the prison. The envelopes are opened and resealed. By the Governor, no doubt. (Hi, Governor!) But James, I know in my heart that you read these pages too. I'm sure of it. Because you're a smart boy. My precious, smart little boy.

Lights out already. I'll write again next week.

This is your father, signing off with much love.

BIOGRAPHY

Deborah Sheldon is an award-winning author from Melbourne, Australia. She writes short stories, novellas and novels across the darker spectrum of horror, crime and noir. Some of her titles include the novels *Body Farm Z, Contrition* and *Devil Dragon*; the novellas *Thylacines* and *The Long Shot*; and collections *Figments and Fragments: Dark Stories* and the award-winning *Perfect Little Stitches and Other Stories*. Her work has been shortlisted for numerous Aurealis and Australian Shadows Awards, long-listed for a Bram Stoker, and included in 'Best of' anthologies. Other credits include TV scripts such as *Neighbours*, feature articles, non-fiction books, stage plays and award-winning medical writing. Visit Deb at http://deborahsheldon.wordpress.com

ADRIAN BALDWIN (COVER ARTIST)

Adrian is a Mancunian now living and working in Wales. Back in the 1990s, he wrote for various TV shows/personalities: Smith & Jones, Clive Anderson, Brian Conley, Paul McKenna, Hale & Pace, Rory Bremner (and a few others). Wooo, get him! Since then, he has written three screenplays—one of which received generous financial backing from the Film Agency for Wales. Then along came the global recession which kicked the UK Film industry in the nuts. What a bummer! Not to be outdone, he turned to novel writing—which had always been his real dream—and, in particular, a genre he feels is often overlooked; a genre he has always been a fan of: Dark Comedy (sometimes referred to as Horror's weird cousin). *Barnacle Brat* (a dark comedy for grown-ups), his first novel won Indie Novel of the Year 2016 award; his second novel *Stanley Mccloud Must Die!* (more dark comedy for grown-ups) published in 2016 and his third: *The Snowman And The Scarecrow* (another dark comedy for grown-ups) published in 2018. Adrian Baldwin has also written and published a number of dark comedy short stories. He designs book covers too—not just for his own books but for a growing number of publishers. For more information on the award-winning author, check out: https://adrianbaldwin.info/

DEMAIN PUBLISHING

To keep up to-date on all news DEMAIN (including future submission calls and releases) you can follow us in a number of ways:

BLOG:
www.demainpublishingblog.weebly.com

TWITTER:
@DemainPubUk

FACEBOOK PAGE:
Demain Publishing

INSTAGRAM:
demainpublishing